W9-BZR-666

DATE DUE

E
Mon   Moncure, Jane Belk
My "w" sound box

ENCYCLOPAEDIA BRITANNICA
EDUCATIONAL CORPORATION
310 S. Michigan Avenue • Chicago, Illinois 60604
85368

My **W** Sound Box

by Jane Belk Moncure

illustrated by Linda Sommers

THE CHILD'S WORLD

MANKATO, MN 56001

Library of Congress Cataloging in Publication Data

Moncure, Jane Belk.
  My w sound box.

  (Sound box books)
  SUMMARY: A little girl fills her sound box with many
words beginning with the letter "w".
  [1. Alphabet] I. Sommers, Linda. II. Title.
III. Series.
PZ7.M739Myw   [E]   78-8614
ISBN 0-89565-046-0 -1991 Edition

My "w" Sound Box

(''wh'' sound included)

Little  had a

"I will find things that begin with my 'w' sound," she said.

"I will put them into my sound  box."

Just then her wildcat   jumped on her
shoulder.

Did she put the
wildcat into her
box?   She did.

She put her wand in, too.

7

Little **w** put on her witch's cape and witch's hat.

Then she went for a walk in the woods.

She found a woodpecker

and wiggly worms.

Did she put the woodpecker and
the wiggly worms into her box? She did.

Little W found a weasel.
He wiggled into the box
as quick as a wink because
a wolf was after him.

box

Little caught the wolf.

Did she put the wolf into the box? She did.
But first, she waved her wand. "Be good,
Wolf," she said.

Little W walked to a well.

She drank some water from the well.
The wolf, the woodpecker, the wiggly

worms and the weasel drank water, too.

"This may be a wishing well," said Little .

So she wished,

"I wish I had something bigger for my things!"

Little W found a wheelbarrow!

"Whee!"
she said.

She wheeled the wheelbarrow . . .

up and down a winding road to the water.

"Let's wade in the water," she said.

But the wolf, weasel, woodpecker, wildcat and wiggly worms did not want to wade! They watched.

"Wow," said a walrus. . .

"What a wacky witch."

"You look wacky too,"

said Little W: "You have

whiskers."

18

Little  put the walrus into the box.

The walrus winked
at the wolf!

box

Little W went back to the water and saw waves! Then she saw

a whale!
The whale whistled.

"I wish
I could put the whale
into my box," said Little
"But he is too big!"

Little  found a

wagon,

a big wagon!
Big enough for a whale!

She put all her things into the wagon
and walked into . . .

a wall!

What was behind
the wall?

24

"Whoopee!" whooped the woodpecker when he saw . . .

watermelons!

"Let's have a watermelon party,"

said Little

And they did.

watermelons

wheelbarrow

wiggly
worms

water

wishing well

wall

whale

walrus

wildcat

wolf

weasel

wagon

27

Can you read these words with Little  ?

window

watch

woman

web

wallet

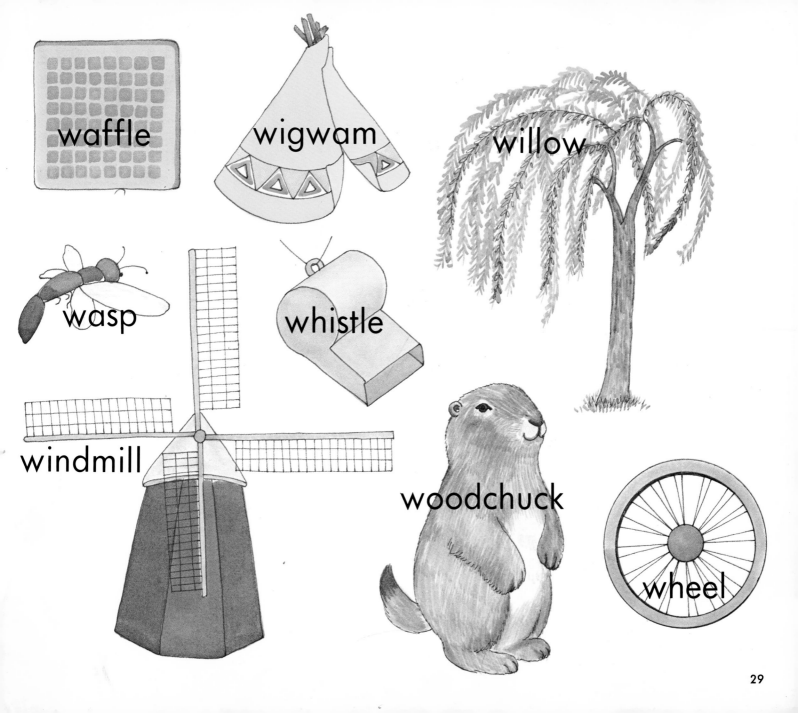

waffle

wigwam

willow

wasp

whistle

windmill

woodchuck

wheel

29